To the dreamers of our world
never give up on your dreams, because dreams do come true.
Mr. Sunny Sunshine and smile machines were just dreams.

Today I've brought these dreams true.
Keep believing in yourself and follow your heart filled dreams,
you'll never know how far your dreams may possibly take you.

Yours truly, Prince of Happiness... King of Smiles.
Dwayne S. Henson

Copyright © 2006 by Dwayne Henson.   574404

ISBN: Softcover   978-1-4257-0004-1
           Hardcover   978-1-4257-3487-9
           EBook   978-1-4691-2846-7

Print information available on the last page.

Rev. date: 03/28/2019

To order additional copies of this book, contact:
Xlibris
1-888-795-4274
www.Xlibris.com
Orders@Xlibris.com

Discover the inspirational magic created from smiles through the guidance of Mr. Sunny Sunshine.

Smile Machines
Written and Illustrated
by
Dwayne S. Henson

Smile Machines! Smile Machines! What are they and what do they do? I would gladly like to provide you with a lesson or two.

Smile Machines! First I like to build them, test them, and name them too, before I show and share my creative inventions with you.

Now come this way I have plenty to show you today.

This is one of my smile machines, it travels kind of slow, but I can bulldoze my way carrying lots of smiles through rough and tough areas where other smile machines can't go. I call this vehicle my Smile Bulldozing Machine.

With this smile machine I can travel through lots of snow, up or downhill. Now watch me go, as I travel fast downhill through the snow. I call this vehicle my Smile Snowmobile.

With this smile machine I can carry a very, very large load of smiles from one place to another. When I need to unload them, all I will need to do is to pull this lever. Here goes! I'm unloading all of these smiles right here just for you. I call this vehicle my Smile Dump Truck.

As you can see with this smile machine I can flatten everything on the road that's in front of me. Squish! Squish! Coming through as I flatten lots of smiles as I travel through. I call this vehicle my Steam Rolling Smile Machine.

With this smile machine I can pick up and move smiles very carefully one by one. I think I need to move this one blue smile just a little over to the left before I release it. I call this vehicle my Smile Crane Machine.

If one of my smile machine vehicles happen to break down, then I can just drive by with this handy vehicle and pick it up, and then take it back to my shop so that I can fix it up. I call this handy vehicle my Smile Tow Truck.

With this smile machine I can travel by floating on top of the sea. Now with a push of a button I'll begin to travel real fast as I splash, splash, splash through the water. I call this vehicle my Smile Speedboat.

With this smile machine I can travel under the sea, I wonder what would I see? Maybe lots of smiles or some hidden treasure maybe? I call this vehicle my Smile Submarine.

This smile machine doesn't have a motor, so I have to wind it up. It moves kind of fast, but the windup power doesn't last. Beep! Beep! Coming through. I call this vehicle my Windup Smile Road Machine.

This smile machine was built to fly; today I think I'll give it a try. Here goes! "Look!" I'm flying high over the clouds in the sky. I call this vehicle my Double Wing Single Propeller Flying Smile Machine.

This smile machine runs on a railroad track it goes Choo! Choo! I can even pick up and carry a load of smiles in the back. I call this vehicle my Smile Choo! Choo! Train.

This smile machine is aimed to the moon. After I make a quick countdown I will go zoom!!! as I'll head on a journey straight to the moon. I call this vehicle my Rocket Power Smile Moon Machine.

This smile machine I just invented, I'm not quite sure how to start it up to make it go. I think I need to pull this red lever first. Ooops! "Oh no!" I think I should have pulled the blue lever marked go.

Well, as you can see from this lesson today, smile machines resemble and work just like some of the helpful vehicle that we see around us in the world today. Smile machines; however assist in a slightly different kind of a helpful way.

As I float down I begin to wonder, what could I or would I ever do without the aid of my smile machines? They help me in so many ways such as; if I need to share a smile or provide some inspiration to someone somewhere, I can just use a smile machine to help me travel there. If the destination is far across the sky, I can just use a smile machine that can fly.

When it comes to providing fun, smiles, entertainment and inspiration too, that's what I create smile machines to help me to do. That's why I'll always keep building them, testing them and sharing them with you.

With a little imagination maybe you can create a smile machine too. If you do I would gladly test it for you. So long for now, as you can see I have lots of testing ahead of me.

A special offer from
the author / illustrator of the
Mr. Sunny Sunshine books
Dwayne S. Henson

← Here's my special offer. Two preschool educational books combined in one at one regular sales price.

For more information on this offer and other Mr, Sunns Sunshine books Contact Xlibris at: 1-888-792-4272 www.Xlibris.com/DwayneHenson

Dwayne S. Henson
Creator of Mr. Sunny Sunshine™

My gift that I would like to share with others is to inspire those who are in need of a smile and to educate others of the positive inspirational value that smiles provide in our society.

With Mr. Sunny Sunshine™ as my tool in this never ending educational smile-based journey. I aim to demonstrate how smiles can be utilized in so many positive encouraging ways such as to inspire, motivate, educate as well as to entertain. How Mr. Sunny Sunshine™ creates smiles and shares them with others, I truly believe, are some of the fascinating trademark dynamics of this inspiring smile making concept.

As you may come to discover there's more inspirational magic behind a smile than what we generally see.

From this unique unit of books you'll learn how and why Mr. Sunny Sunshine™ took it upon himself to create more smiles and inspiration all over the world. Along with this you'll also be provided with a one-of-a-kind, entertaining, smile-based education and much, much, more.

There's a lot to uncover and learn about a smile. I invite you to journey along to see how truly motivating a smile can be.

I certainly hope you enjoy my Mr. Sunny Sunshine™ books as much as I did creating them for others to share. I look forward to creating lots more smiles for many of years to come.

Sincerely, Dwayne S. Henson... Prince of happiness, King of smiles.

Printed in the United States
By Bookmasters